F TO S JOURNEY

IF YOU ARE DETERMINED YOU CAN

DEVIKASIVAGANGA

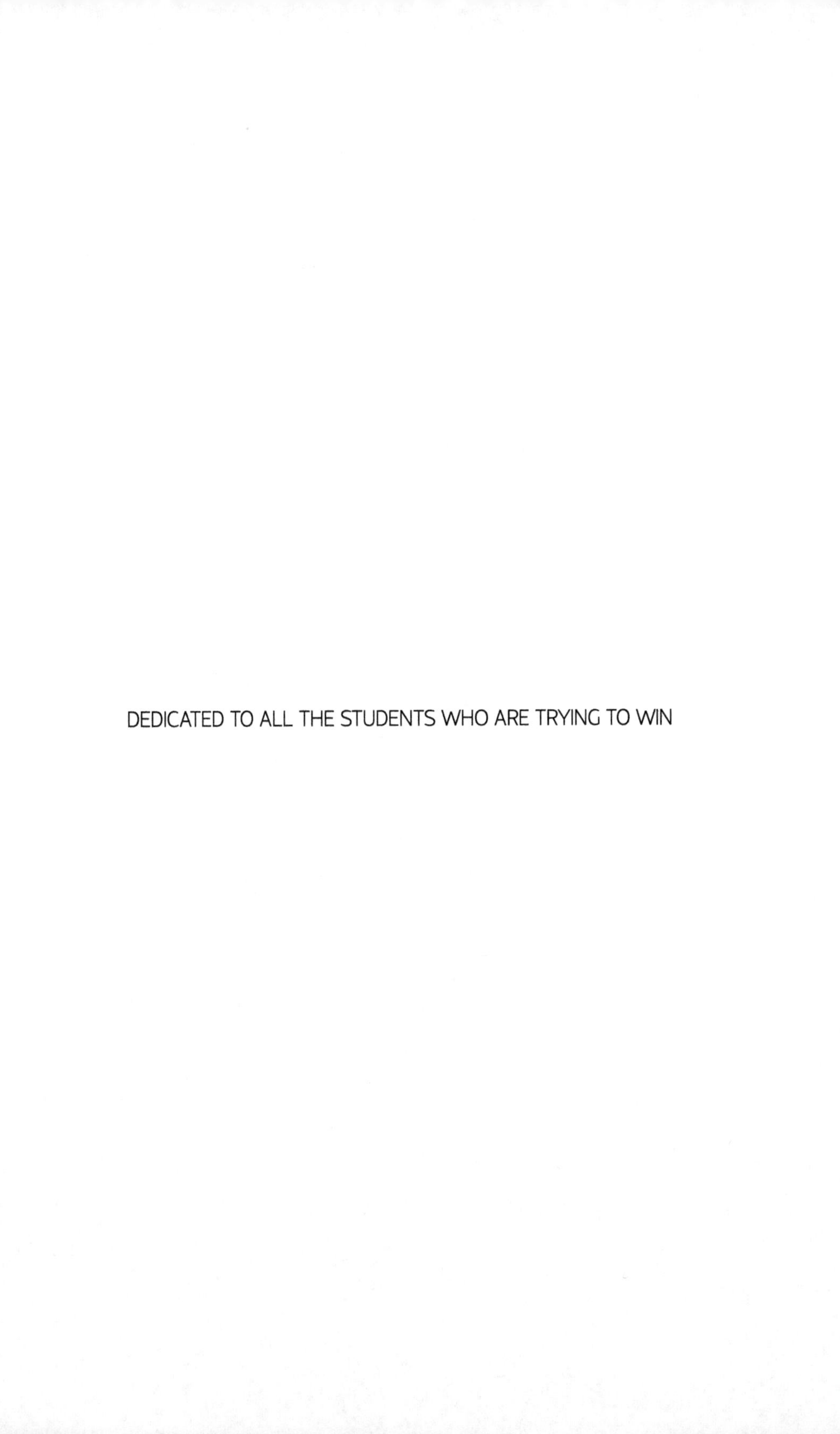

DEDICATED TO ALL THE STUDENTS WHO ARE TRYING TO WIN

Contents

Preface

I STARTED TO WRITE THIS BOOK WHEN I KNOW ABOUT THE CHILDREN WHO ARE TRYING THEIR BEST TO WIN IN A WORLD FULL OF COMPETITION

Prologue

''I will not study '' said kenzo
''You will'' a girl replied

CHAPTER ONE

Introduction

KENZO: born in 1998 October 23

Kenzo was a lower-class family member. His father was a taxi driver and his mother is a babysitter. Kenzo was in 8th standard now. He doesn't know how he came to this high because he is a naughty boy in the school his principal calls him every day and scolds him. Although his teachers like him very much he likes the school . He is studying in a private school his parents are working hard to pay his fees

CHAPTER TWO

Kenzo's words

''I will not study even if you are paying my school fees''
Kenzo said to his parents
His father became angry when he heard this he scolded him. Without any reaction to his father's words, he went to sleep. On lying on the bed he thinks about starting a business because he doesn't want to study anymore, going on thinking he fell asleep. when he woke up the next morning he found a new book on his study table he moved towards it and take a look and went to get ready. He was almost ready to go to school his mother packed a hot pack and gave it to Kenzo.

CHAPTER THREE

AT SCHOOL

Today we are starting our new chapter in physics, don't we?

at that time someone came

"Oh it's a new student " everyone murmured

"Here we have our new student" the teacher told

child, please introduce yourself teacher told the new guy

Student: Hello, my name is Liam nice to meet you I'll be your good friend. Thank you

Teacher: you can go to your place Liam

teacher continued her teaching Kenzo was playing with the paper piece and throwing it to Liam. Liam doesn't told anything when the bell rang teacher went out of the class Liam rushed to go near Kenzo he went and hold his hands

Liam: Hi hello I am Liam what;s your

Kenzo: Kenzo

Liam; ok Kenzo I warn you don't ever do this again if you do it I will kick you out of the class

from that day onwards they both become enemies in all exams, Liam got high marks whereas Kenzo lose his marks Liam teases him whenever he gets time.

CHAPTER FOUR

PRINCIPLE'S UNEXPECTED WORDS

In the middle of the year principal called Kenzo to the professor's room and asked him to leave the school because they told him that they can't afford a boy like this when he heard that tears started to fall down from his small eyes he ran towards his mother " I am sorry" he told he didn't say anything else he ran to his room and locked the door he looked out from his window sunlight made a shadow of him behind. The leaves started to move because of the wind. He fainted

when he opened his eyes he was in the hospital bed, his mother holding his hand "am I too bad " Kenzo asked

"son, no you are not it's okay your father arranged a new school for you you can start going after 1 week" mother told

Kenzo smiled at her

but he is not happy enough

1 week passed,

he forget about all the things that happened he was happy he is getting ready to go to a new school his mother called him and told him that " its a new beginning" he promised that he will be a good boy

when he reached the new school his new classmates welcomed him happily

on the starting day itself, he got a new friend named Siva they become best friends after all kenzo was an average student Siva helped him to study. Kenzo went to libraries every day read books and played games with Siva now he is really changed. He studied hard and achieved good grades.

• 5 •

GETTING SICK

YEARS WENT OFF,

Now he was a college student but an unexpected thing happened to him he become sick for months during his finals he was not able to attend lectures and not able to study anything he is not able to take the finals when he recovered from the sickness he gets to know that he was failed at college and never be accepted to anywhere it was a trgedy in his life because if he wrote the exam he might get a good job and salary he dreamt of becoming a good son and taking care of his parents but now he was not able to do it

CHAPTER SIX

A GIRL'S ARRIVAL

He moved from there he stands at the edge of a bridge and started looking at the water he saw himself in the glazing water suddenly a girl came near him and hold his hands pull him down and asked '' hey what are you going to do I am here to help you death can't solve your problems the girl must be overthinking it ''I am not going to do anything that you said I just looked at the water Kenzo replied

girl: are you stupid why are you standing on the edge and looking into the water what if you slip

Kenzo: it will not happen

Kenzo asked the girl to come with him the girl followed him

Kenzo: what's your name

girl: Laira, and what's your's

Kenzo: Kenzo

Laira: Kenzo come let's go to a tea shop

Laira asked about Kenzo he told her everything that happened

what if I help you Laira asked

Kenzo: how? I know I won't get succeeded in my life because I am a failure

Laira: no, you are not I warn you don't ever repeat that word, by the way, what you like to do

Kenzo: I liked to do business when I was young but now I don't know what to do

Liara and Kenzo talking to each other Laira told to Kenzo to start a business Kenzo started to make some money by doing part-time job and Laira used her salary to help him both tried so hard and started a business Kenzo gave a surprise to Laira he named the company as 'Kenli group' it was perfume company at first it was a failure trying the products they made was getting into the popularity and was loved by the customers with the money they earned Laira and Kenzo started to build branches all over the world kenli group started to get popular and everyone started to love their product Kenzo's parents become so happy to see him like this they exported their product all over the world and company gets high ratings and reviews but the fact that one day Liam came to Kenzo and asked him to give a position in his company so Kenzo kind heartily gave him a position as Laira's personal assistant he made Siva as the head of one of the branches of Kenli group Kenzo and Laira become so happy because of their hard work they made this

now Kenzo was the main head of the Kenli group and Laira was the CEO of the Kenli group

EVERYONE CAN BECOME SUCCESSFUL IN LIFE LIKE KENZO ALL YOU WANT TO DO IS FIND THE ABILITY IN YOU AND TAKE AN EFFORT AND DO IT.

" "